Other Worlds

The Poetry of

Terry Persun

Three Ravens Publishing
Chickamauga, GA USA

Other Worlds Science Fiction Poetry by Terry Persun

Published by Three Ravens Publishing

threeravenspublishing@gmail.com

P.O. Box 851. Chickamauga, Ga 30707

https://www.threeravenspublishing.com

Credits:

Other Worlds Science Fiction Poetry was written by Terry Persun

ISBN: 978-1-951768-38-6

Acknowledgements

Published in Magazines

Big Bang — *Xanadu*

Cryogenic Heartbreak — *AntipodeanSF*

Glitch — *AntipodeanSF*

Missing Mother — *The Raven's Perch*

New World — *The Raven's Perch*

Planet Seven — *The Raven's Perch*

Rocket — *AntipodeanSF*

Space Station Interlude — *AntipodeanSF*

The End — *Minotaur*

Waterworld — *Space and Time* also nominated for the *Rhysling Award* in SF Poetry

Published in Chapbooks or Collections

Big Bang — *Glimpses*
Shut-Down — *Barn Tarot*
Technology — *Sentences*
Trip — *Sentences*
Up for Discussion — *Sentences*

Table of Contents

EARTH BEFORE

Terry Persun

Big Bang

Let's name him Adam,
and from him
in all directions—
whatever hits the fan.

Jupiter makes Pluto
look like a boulder.

I've always wondered
how an explosion
like the Big Bang created
Black Holes
that are imploding
within the exploding
universe.

Something's not right

Terry Persun

with this theory.

Now they're telling
us that physics
is different out there.

And here I sit
inside my dream
of self importance
trying to figure out
what my life means
in reference to Adam,
and how his seed
exploded into this
smaller universe,
how I exploded
into living, how
my mind's like
a Black Hole
all these thoughts

are getting sucked into.

Shut-Down

Working with technology,
I notice what motors
my life along its conveyor
of stubbed toes and held hands.
I listen to the feedback circuits,
the click of limit switches,
the buzz and whir
that signals change.

But as the work wears down
the gear teeth,
as motors short and conveyors slow,
how does production continue?

At the end, I perform regular
error-checks, test circuits for wear,
try to manage a soft shut-down.

Other Worlds

Online

I don't have to leave
my desk for anything
but to take a piss.

I collect data, analyze,
write, talk to co-workers,
read mail, print, sort,
stack, delete. My job

has become a large-screen TV,
a stereo sound system,
a keyboard with F keys
for fuck this and fuck that.

I am monitored: How long
has the computer been on?
Am I typing or reading?

Collecting files? Transferring?
The computer clicks away
like a Chinese torture.

I place a brick over the keyboard.
It slips down. Nothing
but spaces appear on the screen.
I hunch lower onto the floor,
in the corner, next to the open
window.

Technological Assistance

I can see what's in the refrigerator
        from my cell phone.

My car drives me to work and picks
me up
        floors are cleaned robotically
        dinner warmed before I get
        home.

I don't have to get up to operate the
television
        can see into the garage or out
        back
        using my watch
        my tablets or computer.

Centrally located devices answer my questions
      remind me of appointments
      suggest activities for evenings
      checks my bank account
      and secures the house.

I've forgotten how to look things up on my own
      where my wife and kids are off
      to
      what time of day or day of
      week
      how old I am unless I ask
      and desire doesn't come around
      nothing matters any more.

Technology

My car owns the house.
I am caught in the web.
Passive lights don't blink.
I want no more messages.
Threaten the electric company.
Make them shut up.

This is a crash test.
My limits are overflowing.
Ground water relaxes.
Energy produces sparks.
Forever falls between the cracks.
Hear the motors hum.

I force myself to sleep.
Could I turn everything off?
No one knows the answers.

It doesn't matter anymore.
Let's run from ourselves.
We have already disappeared.

Technauseous

Texts from my phone this Tuesday:
Car: Oil change due.
Dishwasher: Washing cycle complete.
Refrigerator: Ice cube tray is full.
Daughter: Will be home late.
Car: Left rear tire needs air.
Coffee shop: Tuesday special, your favorite.
Work: 9:00 meeting postponed until 9:30.
Washer: Replace hot water hose.
Wife: Pick up coffee and meet me… you know where.
Phone company: Your invoice is available for payment.
I turn off my phone, buy coffee. I know where to meet.

Other Worlds

Terry Persun

Up for Discussion

The countdown has begun.
It reads red, then blue.
Numbers do not matter.
Timing means everything.
Yellow tides roll in.
Fish celebrate their astrologies.

A name exists for all this.
Words don't work, though.
Sound isn't upset enough.
Grind it into obscurity.
Pretend it's real.
Ground zero does not exist.

The apocalyptic timer stops.
How does it end?
Breathe in the cruel idea.

Harbor the ship of crying.
Wait here for the end.
Everything is up for discussion.

Trip

I speak through the body.
Tenderness speeds fear.
It's a long road, a short trip.
I cry out with my hands.
I'm leaving now.
It's time to go.

Nature blurs out the window.
Definition disappears.
Details refuse to be heard.
I am separated from the world.
Speed is the barrier.
Jumping off could be dangerous.

Time and motion rejoin.
Have I changed?
Outside, again there are edges.

There are beginnings.
There are endings.
The world has returned.

Selection

Just because there's water
and a semblance of breathable air,
ground, mountains, deserts,
a variety of plants, and even animals,

doesn't mean it's habitable.

Biology is fragile and vulnerable,
susceptible to viruses, diseases,
allergies never been exposed to

to the detriment of the individual.

Volunteers still lined up for miles
outside the registration building,
knowing only a few would be
selected,

not necessarily the strongest or
brightest,
but according to some chosen
combination

that had the best chance of survival.

Nothing anyone could do, say, or pay
could alter the seemingly arbitrary
decision as to who to send skyward

never to be seen again.

CLONE

Terry Persun

Matter

I'm going to say this clearly:
I am small and insignificant
except to my self. The universe
doesn't care about me as an
individual.
I am a laboratory curiosity.
The universe doesn't even know
I exist as I believe I do.
All the philosophers in the world
could not know what the universe
knows.
And yet, I find it worthwhile
to do things that represent me
as though I matter.

Clone

Look-alikes are not act-alikes.
Don't assume equal influences.
Decades adjust your attitudes.
Training stretches intuition.
The riotous moon screams.
Doctor Perfect explodes.

Craters engulf strained ideas.
Parents may be the answer.
Childhood alters brain cells.
Deliberately make a choice.
Share a dwelling not an existence.
Don't stare into my eyes.

Changes are only the beginning.
Have you ever argued with yourself?
When you die, you carry on.

Splitting your soul is a mistake.
It's not really you!
It's not really you.

What We Truly Are

Scientists do not speak of it
and cannot formulate it
into the theories of divided-by's
they use to dissect
and therefore claim
the world, piece by piece.

Materialists have no way to value it
because it cannot be weighed
or measured into the dimensions
of their world. It cannot be
photographed.

What we truly are is not really
a part of anything.
It adds up to more
than the sum of us,

more than what we can give away,
and only through death
do we learn of its value at all.

Clone Answer

Demons stalk the living.
Life's contrasts waken the spirit.
It appears we know what we're doing.
But with distance we look random.
For all the holy texts, no promises
have been kept.
If we knew what we were doing, we'd
just do it.

Snow whitens the air we breathe.
Sound limits our perceptions.
The bell rings and we become dogs.
Let us not forget about those demons.
We have stolen the dark coat.
The sun forgets to hand over the good
luck.

Mankind believes it rules.
Why would anyone tell the truth?
Happiness hears its own words,
nothing else.
We hardly listen deeply anymore.
This existence started with fear.
We've backed ourselves into a corner.

The Code

Once it was cracked,
all hell broke loose.
The message in our DNA
claimed we were eternal,
but why believe that?
A misinterpretation?
It's happened before.

We came from somewhere
that's not Earth. So we decide
to thrust ourselves into the abyss,
searching for home. We know
it's there, just not here.
We take on a new identity:
orphans of the universe,
longing for our natural parents,
our siblings, a hidden beginning.

One cracked code and suddenly
we don't know ourselves, we're lost.

Terry Persun

SPACE

Terry Persun

Rocket

suit up
climb in
set course
check systems
wait…wait

great pressure
difficult breathing
shake, rattle
another push
speed adjust

check systems
call ground
go weightless
recheck course
wait…wait

Goodbye Sun, Goodbye Moon

It's not in the blink
    of an eye—
    a supernova.
Generations can suffer
    slow change,
    adapting, dying off
    without knowing.

Eventually the world
    is scorched,
    the moon's ash,
    people gone.

Nothing except the discarded.

Centuries before, the planning
    started with fits

and political starts.
The chosen planned to keep living.
Where would they go?
Spewed from the planet,
seeds in all directions.

Space Station Interlude

manual adjustments
connect, clamp
secure attachment
open hatch
join crew

complete experiments
log findings
eat, exercise
sleep, work
again…again

check systems
reenter rocket
set course
going home
can't wait

Terry Persun

Weightless

I am not substance. I can't feel
my bulk, my hands, my mind.
Limbs float loosely. A drop
of water could kill me, I am
so fragile. And my bones,
I can feel them weakening,
my muscles atrophy, hearing
and sight change, become shallow.

This tin can I'm traveling
inside is on a generational
journey—I have no home,
will never have a home
again. My past becomes
invisible, my future unknown,
empty for now, weightless.

Terry Persun

Glitch

Billions of bytes of data pass
     through the ships cables
     the electronics hardware
     for decades or centuries.

We're all encased in pods
     of treated and frozen stasis
     waiting for the opening door
     to allow us to live again.

Without a thought we agreed
     and were sent away forever
     wishing to be the first
     to find something new.

Yet everything could end early
     a mistake in programming

parameters changing
one small glitch.

Cryogenics

I
How many millions? Slow death
hugs the coldest brain,
hands placed—like the dead—
across the chest. Waiting
stretches in miles, not minutes,
for distance is also measured
in years. Light, in some far
tunnel of a solar system,
gropes outside our rocket's
window until…it *is* time.

Dependent on electronics
millions of years old to awaken,
warm, our brains into activity,
out of our sloth and into what?
The cold hull of an empty ship.

What can be done, is done.
Cry-o, cry-o, cry-o genic,
let it open our eyes again,
strain to see where we've come
from, where we nearly forgot.
Better that we stayed home.
Even if we are first, who,
back there, remembers us
and does it even matter?

II
The chamber is warm,
yet I hesitate, uneasy
and reticent to step inside
where I'll be flash frozen
like fresh salmon, lobster,
cod. Colder than imagined.

Time doesn't slow, it stops.

Forever lasts longer without
a body—experience halts
leaving memory to play with,
rearrange, but never create
anew. I fear being unfrozen.

A thousand days, or years?
Longer or shorter, nothing
reminds me of my body—
strange, frightening, impossible
to stand, feel, see without
a reference to the physical
world, returned to childhood
I must relearn everything.

Upload Download

Technology races forward
      changing adapting and evolving
      yet I've been in space for
      decades
      comfortable and alone.

My existence depends
      on uploading and downloading
      moving data from one old
      device
      to another then back.

I am moved from one place to another
      from my home planet
      to another distant island
      lodged in the dark sky.

Will another trained person surpass
        my exploratory voyage
        overcome my ancient ship
        and go on ahead without me?

Like a graveyard leaves the discarded
        corpses in the wake of the
        living
        will someone explore light
        years
        ahead after I've given up my
        life.

Abort

Something is terribly wrong
my childhood is recalled
my situation is critical
and I'm a million miles
deep into the galaxy.

Turning around is impossible
yet my ship recommends
that I abort the mission
without explanation
as to what can be done.

A haystack would be easier
to target on Earth
than a planet in the galaxy
yet choice has been deleted
and nothing but hope left.

If I take the ship off autopilot
        steer toward my destination
        while taking short naps
        or going cryogenic
        intermittently
        how far off course could I be?

Options are minimal in such situations
        and I'm not trained to be
        creative
        but my faith reminds me
        that when events are out of my
        hands
        let life choose what it will be.

Cryogenic Heartbreak

Everything is frozen but my heart
    my brain only slowed
    my blood on call
    and my functions waiting.

My heart burns bright in winter
    which could never stop
    me from loving the life
    that will return eventually.

Alone has new meaning when frozen
    into a block on a ship
    sailing through space
    until some unknown time.

Childhood remains through it all
    the torment and beauty

on hold for how long
before freed once again.

In rotation are thoughts and feelings
unable to express for now
waiting for the time when they can
driving me crazy in constant
repose.

Will any of us be the same when warmed
and placed on another planet
that may not understand us
and which we don't understand.

I pray for an end to this stable state
when movement is essential
and memory can be increased
with actual experiences.

Autopilot

I know very little about how things
work
    although once a long time ago
    the nuances were taught me
    preparing for the final moment.

It's been years since I've had to recall
    trajectories from a place unseen
    toward a place slowly coming
    toward me at a million miles
    and hour.

Studying ship documents doesn't help
    if my confidence is shaken
    if my nerves are on edge
    if my memory doesn't serve
    me.

So I rely on a system that was made
years ago
        that has been operating since
        takeoff
        and has not failed for longer
        than I should have lived in the
        first place.

Monitors

At last the light from a sun—
    years traveling between
    them—penetrates the shield
    of thick glass dimming
    the glimmer of my console.

Monitor lights are part of my life,
    my only light, my body's
    explanation—indicating
    temperature, pressure,
    heartbeat, circulation.

As I ready the pod for landing
    the brightness of this sun
    scares me and the loss
    of my monitors' glow
    tears at my soul.

Weapons Alert

The last alarm I expect to hear
        is sounding its deep
        grinding tone into my ear
        and I can't remember how
        to turn the damned thing off.

I glare at my monitors and video
screens
        searching for what might
        appear
        an alien ship or asteroid
        near enough to sound the alarm
        or might it be nothing at all.

A glitch in the system would mean
worse
        danger than an actual attack

since this one warning
would indicate that my systems
are beginning to fail.

I rack my brain and memory
searching
for what to do after all this time
traveling through open space
without a single concern
but to survive until landing.

And now this alarm scares me awake
leaves me wondering how
well researched any of this
could have been seeing that
I am the first to wander this far.

Missing Mother

I give in to the vibration
and rumble, not to mention
the horrendous pressure
tearing my teeth out.

Like a carnival ride,
a twist and shift in directions
that shock my body alive
changes my equilibrium.

Born and raised on ship,
the outside frightens
me to the core and bone—
so much space and freedom.

I belong inside the womb
of Mother Ship, long

for protective walls,
the humming of engines.

I will forever feel
ripped from my home
and live only to return—
God is my Mother.

Terry Persun

OTHER PLANETS

Terry Persun

Lab Stats

We've already found life
    the thousandth time
    in space floating
    but microscopic.

What did we expect to find
    intelligence
    DNA like ours
    a companion race?

Microscopic life doesn't mean us
    anything like us
    but another
    nothing we understand.

What if we're alone universally
    we have no relatives

nothing to conquer
does it end there?

Surveillance

How could they know
        with their technology-lite
        that we are watching them
        to decide which direction
        they might turn
        once we invade their space?

Our experiments seem cruel
        to them, yet do nothing
        that would harm them
        in the least. They are
        so delicate.

But they are also animals
        to one another and spread
        that violence much further
        than we could or would do.

Terry Persun

Let this be a lesson
        to them that they are not
        the most advanced race

in the universe
        or even the galaxy

and perhaps should not live.

New World

We are here. We made it.
Yes, the Earth is gone,
but we—the lucky and best—
have come to this place.

We few out-tested, out-bid,
outsmarted the unchosen
to spend years in storage,
months in preparation,
grueling as it has been,
and days arriving on lands
that are new, to plant and harvest,
hunt and fish, to live by the hands
we had forgotten were our own.

The rest of our lives we'll toil,
suffer, and survive, then die

no differently and with no more
to show for it, than those
we deemed inadequate.

This Strange Place

The bird lands, the size of an eagle
but not an eagle. Head down, it tears
the meat from the ground mammal,
which has the gray fur and body
of a rat—even its hairless tail—
but there are no rats in this far-off
place.

Home is said to be where the heart is,
where you hang your helmet, but my
heart
has been left in another solar system.
No matter how much like Earth,
this grassy plane and blue sky is not
my home.

Each animal, stranger than the next,

is false, dreamlike. Each rock is formed
by an unfamiliar wind. Each plant, unknown
and dangerous. I move forever forward
in another's dream, unable to awaken.

Waterworld

All night, it sloshes in starts
and ends. You learn its sounds:
current shifts, speeds, can almost
hear the fish—if you can call them
fish—passing under your floating
craft, the remains of your spaceship.

Nothing makes sense the way water
begins to. Nothing flies, only swims,
a few feet away, a mile, many miles.
You can hear everything, smell all,
but not see the expanse. Sun reflects,
blinds, makes you wonder if your
eyes
will evolutionize themselves extinct.

Haunting are the sounds unseen,

the life in shadows barely
under the surface. The mind plays
tricks and you begin to add
shapes, horrible and beautiful,
to the movements of things. You
cringe at the thought of killing
what you can't yet see, just
to remain alive, to survive.

Trackbot

All-terrain is assumed
    not guaranteed
    locked in vines
    slipping in powder.

Its job falls short
    yet circuits run
    software purrs
    algorithms calculate.

An inhospitable planet
    breaks through logic
    evaporates common sense
    down an empty hole.

Abandoned and forgotten
    the machine wines

claustrophobia sets in
electronics overheat.

Evil Calling

They are swarms with one mind
knowing everything as it happens.

They are fiber and synapse
waiting for nature to move them.

They sense wind, sun, odor at once
interpreting how to proceed.

They are the planet we've come to
remaining unaware that we might
destroy everything they are
out of our own ignorance.

Peaceful Planet

Unschooled in peace,
we bring weapons
to frighten ourselves
into action and response.

The child misunderstands
the rushing dog, tail flailing.
Music is the sound
we learn to think is music.

Our gift is aggression,
anger in view of silence,
blinded by self-gratification
and utter ignorance.

Can a planet understand more
than what a species knows

about itself and others?
Or is the game almost over?

Zoo

After the crash, they took
me in and saved my life
from pain, scars, memories.
Teammates scattered, body parts
mostly—memory-wiped, foggy
but you can't wipe totally.

From my habitat,
their three-eyed children
stare and point, my heart races
for escape, but to where?
Unfamiliar cities, local wildlife,
and the multi-armed inhabitants
are frightening and dangerous.

Fed and cared for, there's nothing
to experience but sophisticated

toys thrown into my room,
machines that try to teach
a language my mouth can't shape,
understand a life I never wanted
regardless how clean and appropriate.

Planet Seven

The sky is yellow, the grass
blue and red. Photosynthesis
has twisted physics left
of center, stranger than
where it used to reside.
Earth so far away nothing
learned there applies anymore.

The star-bound trip here,
at the very edge of a galaxy
robbed the memory of land,
sea, air with a yellow sun.

In weeks memory and reality
weave together new neurons
that line up together, recalling
joined experiences, emotions

earned through minds not
even from this far off place.

Invasion

On another Earth, the invaders
don't bother to show up, instead
robots shaped like mechanical
monsters grind us up for what?
Food, fuel, mulch for the gardens
they have stolen from us. Not worth
the energy to come in person,
they fly-by, drop their drones
like an insecticide to eliminate
the pests who have made homes
on the last useful planet available
for them to own, to colonize.

EARTH AFTER

Terry Persun

The Assistant

I am the watcher,
the recorder. From wherever
I stand, sit, or lie,
wherever my mind sneaks.
I have been called spy
and peeping Tom.

Someone has to do the dirty work

of taking it all down:
thoughts, emotions, actions,
chemical imbalances.
The job's not at all easy.

Interpretation crawls through,
editorializing finds a way in.

Terry Persun

Translation is necessary more often
than not.

How do I write what bees think?
The buzzing of the greater
metropolis?

What words express properly our
dreams,
meditations, longings, or spiritual
knowing?
This is detailed work and
monotonous.

All Systems Go

Room filled with technicians at
screens
        equipment humming with duty
        bring your child to work day
        explanations tests
        confirmations.

What were they paying attention to
        when so many questions flared
        around everyone's work
        station?

Not a thought slipped from my mind
        as countdown commenced.

The cat somehow scooted outdoors.

Web

My existence,
no matter how
small, is forever
part of the universal,
eternal web
of energy, and
movement of any
kind: mental,
physical, spiritual,
is forever one
with all things
and non-things
lifting and falling
like so many
breaths along
this complex
beingness with which

we all are.

Terry Persun

We Are

not alone in the universe as thought
God did not choose
our species in his image

there are many intelligences

the revelation that we're not first
crippled our egos our governments
our meanings our value

everything tied to perception

being the only intelligence
what conceit a false pedestal
how crude of our barbaric selves

Aliens

They have arrived in force,
the sky belongs to them beyond
how it belonged to us. They have
made us feel stupid and unenlightened
with our small accomplishments,
our ancient technologies
as though we haven't moved
beyond the invention of the wheel.

Our God, after all our years of
worship,
did not place us on a pedestal,
but them instead. We are humbled
to the core, lost in our arrogance
and self-appointed self-importance.

We are not kings or queens

of the universe. They have
done, already and for years,
what was once our job to do.
They wish to make our lives
easier, take away every disease,
feed us when we are hungry,
shelter us when we are cold, love us.

All our struggles, wars, education,
spiritual growth, brilliance has carried
us
to this one end, this one realization:
We have become nothing more than
pets.

The End

In the future we do not die.
Our lives become the same
day after day. We have a million
years to write that novel,
so we don't write it,
a thousand years to fall in love,
so we become bored
with our penises and vaginas.
We realize there is no Heaven
for us now. We are like toys
that repair themselves.
If there ever was a God,
we believe He abandoned us
to ourselves, and we no longer
know what to do or think,
we no longer know why
we are even here or what

Terry Persun

it all means.

Immortality

When we live forever, we will
find that at the end of a series
of memories, we all go through
what we've learned to call
an Alzheimer's moment,
which could last years,
like menopause, but then break
into a new, unexpected
personality—a different person.
Perhaps that is all reincarnation
has ever been—the end of one story
and the beginning of another—but
now
there's no need for a second,
third, or fourth body. We hone
the casing we have and keep
it strong, replacing elements—

hips, knees, hearts, piece
by piece until we are truly
not flesh and blood in the same way
that we think of it now,
but grown in a lab, in a cleanroom.
Over and over, we get to live,
only this time with some sense
of who we were, our histories
become monstrous in size
and complexity. We become gods
in many senses of the word.
But we are fooled in the end.
The Earth does not live forever.
In our haste to become immortal
we have neglected our mother,
and when she dies she takes us
with her into the oblivion
we tried so hard to escape.

Terry Persun Bio

Terry Persun writes intelligent, tech-forward fantasy and science fiction with clearly drawn characters and thought-provoking themes. His novels have been winners and finalists in over a dozen awards, including a Book Excellence Award winner, a Silver IPPY winner, a New Apple Book Award winner, a Cygnus finalist, and multiple Foreword Book of the Year Award finalists. He has worked as an airborne navigations equipment specialist and electronics engineer and presently freelances for science and technology magazines. You can find out more here: www.TerryPersun.com